Dragonflies with bright blue bellies darted under the apple trees at the far edge of the orchard, traveling from the swamp to the trees and back.

Shawna always wondered about the messages the dragonflies carried. She knew nobody lived in the swamp, nobody *real*, just a made-up king and his court that she and her twin sister Rowan always told stories about. And she knew that dragonflies didn't carry messages. She was ten, after all. She even knew the truth about Santa Claus and everything.

Still, she wondered.

The Dead Sister

Leah Cutter
Copyright © 2016 Leah Cutter
All rights reserved
Published by Knotted Road Press
www.KnottedRoadPress.com

ISBN: 978-1-943663-27-9

Artwork:

© Zulla | Dreamstime.com - Portrait Of The Girl Photo

Cover design and interior © copyright 2016 Knotted Road Press

The Dead Sister

Leah Cutter

Also By Leah Cutter

The Seattle Trolls:
The Changeling Troll
The Princess Troll

The Shadow Wars Trilogy:
The Raven and the Dancing Tiger
The Guardian Hound
War Among the Crocodiles

The Clockwork Fairy Kingdom:
The Clockwork Fairy Kingdom
The Maker, the Teacher, and the Monster

Contemporary Fantasy:
Of Myst and Folly
Siren's Call
When the Moon Over Kualina Mountain Comes
Zydeco Queen and the Creole Fairy Courts

The Cassie Stories:
Poisoned Pearls
Tainted Waters
Spoiled Harvest

The Chronicles of Franklin:
The Popcorn Thief
The Soul Thief

The Dead Sister

Leah Cutter

Knotted Road Press

www.KnottedRoadPress.com

The Dead Sister

I

Dragonflies with bright blue bellies darted under the apple trees at the far edge of the orchard, traveling from the swamp to the trees and back.

Shawna always wondered about the messages the dragonflies carried. She knew nobody lived in the swamp, nobody *real*, just a made-up king and his court that she and her twin sister Rowan always told stories about. And she knew that dragonflies didn't carry messages. She was ten, after all. She even knew the truth about Santa Claus and everything.

Still, she wondered.

The water at the edge of the swamp looked icky. Bright green slime floated on the top of it, clinging to the cattail reeds growing there. Fat bees with black and yellow fur flew lazily between the stems. Every once in a while, the water burped from one of the stupid fish swimming there, hidden by the slime and dirt.

Despite how it looked, and sometimes smelled like rotting grass, Shawna still loved the swamp. Loved how it rustled to itself at night, the mysterious sounds the wind carried from it. She hoped that they'd have a really, *really* cold winter that year, so that maybe the front part of the swamp would freeze and she could explore it.

No one knew how deep the water in the swamp went. Tommy, from up the road, always told them the ground dropped right off and the water went down and down and down. He'd teased Shawna and Rowan about building a platform taller than the three-story farmhouse they lived in so he could dive straight into the water.

Not even the heat of the August afternoon tempted Shawna to go swimming in that water, and she loved to swim. She was a very good swimmer, particularly compared to her sister.

However, that swamp water just looked yucky. And she didn't want to get her clothes dirty, even though she wore an old pair of cutoffs with a faded T-shirt that still had paint stains on it from earlier that summer when she'd been helping Dad paint their shared room a bright, cheery buttercup-yellow.

Still, she *really* wanted to win the game of hide and seek that she was playing with Rowan, Tommy, and the rest of the gang. Hiding down here near the swamp seemed like the perfect place.

Besides, Shawna knew that she'd be safe. She was following the lights, after all.

Not everyone could see the swamp lights, not like her. Rowan thought they were make-believe, like the king and his court. Even Mom didn't like it when Shawna talked about the lights, telling her not to get confused with what was real and what wasn't.

But Shawna could see them. They *were* real. Tiny, off-white lights, like Christmas tree lights that had been turned on for too long, floating between the edge of the water and the land on a long string. They marked the border between the swamp and the orchard.

As long as Shawna stayed on *this* side of the lights, everything would be fine. She could walk much closer to the edge of the swamp than anyone else and still be safe. The lights showed her where the solid ground ended.

It meant she could hide down here next to the swamp, too.

Instead of going to the point where the swamp invaded the orchard, Shawna went around to the left, skirting the water and the tall reeds. She'd always thought that the sharp edge of the swamp was like a fist, shoving its way into the orchard right in the center of what Dad called the back forty. On either side of the invading bulge the swamp was more behaved, pulling back and letting grass and trees grow.

Shawna didn't worry about leaving the farm—Dad and Mom owned all the land around here, including the swamp. Their property went north another mile or so, to the county road that marked the border. Thick, *mean* trees lined the road there, what Dad called a Russian olive, with thorns as long as her palm and silvery-green leaves. Sometimes, in the early summer, when the wind blew just right over the swamp, she could smell the flowers growing there, sweetly dark and foreign.

However, most of the time she could only smell the murky water, the mustiness of the cattails, mingled with the sweetness of the fruity trees, behind her.

Dad had wanted to drain the swamp, get rid of the muck, and expand the orchard. But the government said he couldn't, the water had gotten itself protected as wetlands.

Shawna wasn't exactly sure how that had happened. One year they'd been making plans. Then they next year, they couldn't.

Dad blamed the *damned hippies* who lived at the end of the road.

Shawna tried not to listen when Dad swore like that.

She also figured it was the swamp who had done it. That the swamp itself had sent the king and his messengers to the courthouse all the way down in Indianapolis to make them declare his land sacred.

Rowan didn't believe that at all. She figured the king had *scared* the "damned hippies" into going to court to save the wetlands.

Or maybe it had been a little bit of both.

Shawna walked carefully along the edge of the trees, keeping her eye on the lights, looking for that perfect hiding spot. She knew that Tommy would count to one hundred slowly because he didn't believe in cheating that way. Other ways, sure, but not with the count that someone else could hear. Tommy was sneaky that way.

The grass didn't grow very high here, under the trees. Not enough sunlight. And the water was too close. The few trees that did grow here had muscled their way up, with smooth bark covering their bulging limbs. Fewer dragonflies flew between them. A red-winged blackbird cawed loudly from the swamp—lots of birds had their nests in the swamp.

It made Shawna glad that their homes were protected, now.

Shawna spied a tall stand of dead reeds. Funny, she didn't remember them, and she knew most every inch of the orchard. She'd explored it all, mapped it in her head. Someday, she was going to grow up and be a great explorer and discover new continents and worlds and everything.

Maybe the reeds had been growing and alive, before? Earlier in the summer? And so that was why she didn't remember them as dead? The reeds looked as dry and spindly as if they'd been standing in two feet of snow for most of the winter, the broad, flat leaves shivering in a wind she didn't feel.

The cattail part of the reeds seemed to be missing, too, as though someone had come onto their land and just chopped off the tops, to use them for their own table decorations, like people did in the fall.

That made Shawna mad. No one was allowed onto their land but *family*.

She marched right over to the stand of reeds. The edges shivered. They only came up to her mid-chest. But she could squat down in the center of them and nobody would find her. Her long brown hair, that she wore in two braids, was darker than the faded reeds, but hopefully that wouldn't give her away.

Quickly, Shawna walked past the reeds along the far side of the clump. She needed to see how deep the stand went. It was at least three, maybe four feet wide. The lights marking the border of the swamp bobbed closer than she'd expected, floating just on the other side of the stand of reeds.

It would be the perfect place to hide. Nobody else could get this close to the water's edge, not without falling in.

So Shawna slipped between the tall, dead leaves. "Shhh," she said, shushing them, afraid their rustling would give her away.

She couldn't see the edge of the swamp from deep inside the reeds. But the ground still felt stable enough under her feet. She took one step. Then another. Then a third.

Lights glowed just past where Shawna was about to squat down. She squatted a little and turned, checking behind her.

She couldn't see anything but the reeds. Still, she didn't want Tommy to be able to rush up and find her.

Just one more step…

Water and mud squelched up around her sandals, sliding in between her toes. Shawna bit down on her squeal, not wanting to give her position away. She tried to step back, but found herself slipping instead, her butt landing hard on the cold wet ground.

Then she kept sliding.

The reeds hadn't really been dead, they'd just been playing dead. Now, they pushed her, shoving her into the water. Other reeds waited there, the mean ones, who wrapped themselves around her legs and started pulling her down into the water. The wet smell of the reeds pushed out the more friendly scents of hot sun on the dry grass.

Shawna muffled her cry for help. She didn't want Tommy and the others to accuse her of being scared of the swamp and screaming like a little girl. She also didn't want to lose hide and seek either.

Maybe that was a mistake.

The swamp wasn't letting her go. Water quickly covered her head, warmer than she'd expected.

Her toes tingled, as if minnows nibbled on them. She screamed now, though that just sucked more water into her mouth. It tasted nasty, making her choke and cough and suck more in. She thrashed, trying to break free, get her head back above water.

She just kept sinking. The water itself now sucked her in.

The fairy lights that marked the border swam closer and closer, buzzing like angry bees.

A dark opening followed the lights, like a doorway into night.

Shawna didn't want to go through that door. It wasn't her time, yet. This was wrong.

She kicked her legs hard, stirring up the muck at the bottom of the swamp, making all the water dark and dim. The reeds still had hold of her. They wouldn't let go. The water pushed down on her. Her hands got tangled up in the strings of fairy lights. Fish bit her toes, sending sharp pains through her legs.

Darkness overwhelmed her.

Shawna couldn't breathe. Her chest hurt. Her head swam and she felt woozy.

Dragonflies suddenly flashed above her head, their blue bellies glowing, taking note of her situation.

Shawna reached up and tried to capture one. It easily evaded her clumsy fingers and flew off, leaving her alone in the dark.

Who had they gone to report to? Would they bring help?

Suddenly, Shawna's lungs stopped hurting. Her arms drifted down to her sides. She couldn't raise them. Couldn't wiggle her toes.

Her eyes started to close. She struggled, but she couldn't keep them open anymore.

A deep calm flowed over her, like a warm blanket of night.

There wasn't anything she could do except to lay back and sleep.

Shawna stood by the edge of the swamp, next to the tricksy reeds.

She knew she was dead. She couldn't explain exactly how she knew that. But she didn't feel alive anymore.

Maybe she knew she was dead because despite the darkness, she could still see *everything*. Each apple tree stood distinct and separate from the grass. The stars up above her twinkled in the black sky. It was far past her bedtime, but she no longer felt tired.

Or maybe she knew she was dead because instead of her T-shirt, shorts, and sandals, she was now barefoot and wore a white dress, like what her friend Bridget had worn to her first communion. It flowed down to just past her knees, with long sleeves and a high collar. It glowed slightly in the dark night and it had pretty white ribbons rippling down the skirt. It was a princess dress, more suited to Rowan than Shawna. Still, it was pretty.

Or maybe it was because, for the first time, she could *hear* the swamp whisper and mutter to itself.

She (because Shawna now realized that the swamp was a *she*) sang lullabies over the soft waters to help the reeds grow deep. She blew sweet dreams to the sparrows, juncos, blackbirds, blue jays, robins, and all the other birds who nested deep in her heart. She bristled behind her thorn trees, the guards who protected her northern-most flank from the humans. And she murmured to her messengers, the dragonflies and bees, gnats and wasps, encouraging them to tell her of all the things they'd seen.

Shawna looked through the trees toward the farmhouse where her sister and her mom and her dad still lived. She kind of remembered them kneeling on the spot where she stood now, her mother screaming and crying over her dead body. And how sad her dad had looked. How he'd tucked one of her braids back behind her ear. How tearful Rowan had gotten, as if someone had just destroyed her heart.

All that felt distant. Maybe that was part of being dead, too. But still, Shawna didn't want to remember it, to feel it too closely.

Thinking about Rowan, Shawna realized that she felt connected to her twin. Somewhere deep, below Rowan's dreams, Shawna could reach her, communicate with her, though maybe not with words.

Of course, Rowan, being human and alive, might not remember Shawna talking to her in the morning, might just think they were dreams.

Still, Shawna tried to comfort her sister, to show her the bright lights of the fireflies, the soft song of the swamp, the way the stars whirled overhead.

Rowan followed Shawna for a very short while before she fled back into her own dreams, scared and shaken and crying for Mom and Dad.

Maybe tomorrow night Rowan would draw closer and Shawna would be able to show her more, to tell her not to be scared.

For now…Shawna turned her back on the orchard and everything human and alive and faced the swamp, her new home.

Off in the distance she heard the quiet bells of the court ringing. She knew they rang for her.

Time to go and meet the king.

2

Shawna really wished she didn't have to go back into the water. It still looked yucky. Slime covered the top of it. She didn't want to get her new dress dirty. Or her hair, which had come unbound and now waved loosely down her back. Was there a better way?

As she approached the edge of the swamp, the little fairy lights that marked the border between the land and the water changed. They still looked slightly brown and burned out. But they rearranged themselves. Instead of forming a straight line, baring her way, they broke in two, giving her a path.

As the lights bobbed closer to the surface, they cleared away the muck, holding it back for her. Gratefully, Shawna stepped forward, past the tricksy reeds, into the clear water.

Her bare feet felt gravel, not mud and slime as she stepped down. The water itself was only as warm as Rowan's bathwater

(Shawna always wanted it hotter). Her dress didn't float up, but flowed as easily into the water as she did. So did her hair, sinking down with the rest of her.

Tommy was wrong—the ground sloped away easily, not steeply, from the shore. Shawna took several steps before she paused, looking back, the water tickling her chin. She could see the dark trees, standing with their branches intertwined as if forming a barrier. The grass looked darker too, a thick carpet.

Up above her, more stars whirled than she'd ever seen before. It made her dizzy. But they also made her glad, brightening her heart.

Still, Shawna paused. She couldn't take a deep breath, though that was what her body wanted her to do. It scared her, a little, to stick her head back under the water. She'd drowned there. Had died.

But the king was waiting. And Shawna had always been so very curious about his land.

The swamp paused in her summer song as she considered this new creature.

She didn't like Shawna. Didn't like any humans, dead or alive.

But the swamp wouldn't stop Shawna from entering her lands. Shawna was such a small thing, still so new and young, while swamp herself was so very, very old.

Shawna remembered one of her school lessons, teaching about the Great Lakes, and how much of the ground surrounding the lake had been underwater at one time. Even her dad's farm.

The swamp still remembered that time, when she had been part of a much, much larger body of water. She had held herself true while the rest of the water had allowed itself to be tricked into drying up or been driven underground to lie in wells and hidden lakes.

So Shawna had the swamp's…not permission. More like indifference, that allowed her to enter.

Shawna pretended to take a deep breath, then took that last step down, ducking her head under the water.

It didn't surprise Shawna that she could see under the water. She'd been able to see so much above the water, more than she had when she'd been alive, so of course she should be able to here as well. She was, after all, dead.

The lights continued to form a path for her, leading the way into the darker waters. Shawna was grateful for them, afraid that she'd get lost without them.

Wild weeds grew out of the muck on either side of the lights lining her path. They had long, thin leaves and looked gray-green. They waved back and forth, as if being pushed and pulled by strong water currents. Were they dancing, welcoming her? It made her smile.

A silvery fish as long as her arm darted across the path. Here and gone. The water swirled in its wake, sighing softly.

It surprised her. She'd always thought the fish in the swamp were nasty, mean things. But this fish had seemed elegant racing through the water on its very important journey somewhere. Its color, too, wasn't what she'd expected.

Then she paused, thinking about how big the fish had been. Had she grown smaller? Shrunk when she'd walked into the swamp? She didn't feel tiny. Still she wondered, particularly when she realized the weeds growing on either side of her were taller than her chest, now.

The song of the swamp echoed loudly this far under the water. Shawna felt the notes caressing her bare arms, soothing her skin. The song carried the smell of dusty reeds and wet grass. Yet the song felt more angry, too. The swamp didn't like its current boundaries. So every note pushed and *pushed* at the edges, trying to convert more land into swamp.

The song covered everything else, muting Shawna's world: the colors, the sounds, even the smells.

Or maybe that was part of being dead, that nothing felt or seemed close or immediate anymore.

Shawna made herself start walking again, marching along the path made for her by the lights on either side. She didn't like to think about being dead, about missing her family and the great blue sky above.

Beside the trail, a forest of logs grew, sticking up out of the ground on either side. They were huge: she couldn't have put her arms all the way around a single trunk. Had the woods once foolishly tried to grow in the swamp? Or had the swamp lost her power for a while, and the land had pushed itself in?

No matter. The swamp had drowned those trees, hidden away their view of the sun. The rock and gravel around those stumps had turned to soft ground. It stirred as Shawna passed, a soft sifting sound, reminding Shawna of fallen leaves. She knew that if she walked off the hard path she traveled, the mud would stain her toes, turn her white skin brown.

Just past the collection of logs, a bright white light glowed. As Shawna approached, the glow spread out. The string of lights marking her path faded away, but Shawna knew where she was going, now.

If Shawna had been alive, she would have gasped as she crested the ridge and looked down.

A grand palace lay before her, made of soft pink seashells and hard white rock. Baby blue reeds sprouted out of the walls, waving like fans. Red iron-ore decorated the frames of the many windows and doors. Beautiful gardens of water grasses spread out over the front lawn.

Shawna didn't know where to look first! The palace had three, no, five towers that were the points of the huge building, spread out like the fingers of a hand. The palace itself had two stories in some places, three in others, all topped by a sloped red-clay roof.

She *must* have shrunk when she walked into the water. The swamp wasn't deep enough to cover such a huge building.

It wasn't built like a human palace, stiff and clean. It looked more like it had been grown. The windows weren't lined up, one on top of another. Instead, they were different sizes and shapes: : round windows, square windows, windows as big as double doors, windows not much bigger than a peephole. They were scattered randomly across the walls, as if whenever someone had wanted to look out they'd just punched a hole in the wall. A reflective glass covered all the windows, shining with its own soft blue light.

Would all the light inside the palace be blue because of the windows?

The doors to the palace stood wide open, showing a darkness inside that made Shawna a little uneasy. Up on the second story, between two of the front towers, strung a balcony. Probably for the guards, though no one stood there now.

A school of tiny, brown fish flowed around Shawna. She stopped, startled as they brushed past her. None of the fish were as long as her palm. They seemed to be in an awful hurry, though, as they swam as fast as they could through the open palace door. They carried a lemony scent with them.

Shawna thought for a moment. She'd loved grilled fish when she'd been alive. Now, though it had been hours and hours, she found she wasn't hungry.

She might never be hungry again.

That made her sad.

But she wouldn't be able to meet the king if she wasn't dead.

Shawna also missed being able to breath. It had been so automatic when she'd been alive. She found she could still swallow, however, a big gulp, before she started down the slight hill, toward the gorgeous palace.

Shawna paused in the front entranceway of the palace. The water seemed warmer, here. It smelled darker and sweeter, too, like someone had mixed a trace of buckwheat honey (her favorite kind) in with the water. Large flat stones in all colors of brown and red covered the floor. The ceiling went up for two stories, the walls mostly made from a plain gray stone.

Far above her head, opposite the door, stood another grand opening. At first, she was disappointed that a grand staircase didn't lead up to it.

With a start, she realized that staircases were *human* things.

It wouldn't take much for her to swim up to that second floor. Though she'd been walking like she normally did, her dead body still somewhat weighted, she didn't have to walk. She could swim.

Shawna giggled to herself, the sound echoing in the open space.

That was when she realized the song of the swamp was muted inside the palace. She could barely hear the swamp at all in here.

Were the swamp and the king at war? Did she barely tolerate his place here? It made Shawna uneasy. She almost turned around and walked back out the door.

But she'd always wanted to meet the king, so she drifted further into the entranceway.

Pretty mosaics decorated the nearby walls, done with colorful stones: pictures of fish and reeds, birds and dragonflies, even a mermaid and the ocean.

The little lights that had guided her earlier suddenly sprang up again. They highlighted another door that she hadn't seen earlier. It wasn't made of wood, but of rusted stone and iron. It stood to the right, in the corner.

Shawna swallowed down her disappointment that she wouldn't be swimming up to the top floor. Maybe later she'd have the chance to explore.

The cold smell of rust flowed past her as she went through the door. The corridor seemed so dark after the front entrance. The water here was much colder as well, and she discovered that even though she was dead, she could still get goose bumps across her arms. However, the dark hallway went on only for a short while before it opened up again.

On either side of a set of closed double-doors stood two squat guards. She'd never seen anything like them before! Were they human? She wasn't sure.

The guards barely came up to her shoulders. Everything about them looked squished: their faces were round with red cheeks that stuck out, with pointed chins and noses. They wore tall hats that rode low on their foreheads, as if their bushy black eyebrows held them in place. The hats looked like they were made of black moss, soft to the touch.

Their uniforms looked woven out of reeds, with cattail stripes and yellow-grass skirts. Like her, they were barefoot. They each had swords, the handles sticking up over their shoulders.

Shawna somehow knew the swords weren't just for show: The guards practiced with them and knew how to use them with deadly precision.

The one of the left glared at her. He looked older, with more lines on his face. The one on the right looked younger and said gruffly, "They're waiting for you." He opened the door then stood back at attention, waiting for her to pass.

Shawna hesitated. So the dragonflies *had* reported her death to the king. She wished she could tell Rowan. Maybe she could show her sister, later. In her dreams.

"It'll be all right, miss," the guard who opened the door whispered to her. He seemed the nicer of the two.

"Thank you," Shawna said. She realized it was the first time she'd spoken since she'd died. The words sounded ghostly to her ears, with no breath behind them to make them stronger.

The guards weren't dead, she realized. They weren't…like her.

Even though they looked mostly human, she knew they weren't.

But she wasn't going to be scared of them. Or the king.

Head held high, Shawna walked through the door, and into the court.

The door opened up on the side of the grand hall, not directly opposite the king. Was that to keep him safe? So an army couldn't just swarm in and attack him? There weren't any of the blue-glassed windows either.

Directly above her head stood a balcony. It went all the way around the square room, supported by carved wooden pillars, made to look like they were covered in ivy.

It was the first wood that Shawna had seen. Didn't wood rot under the water?

Maybe it was a sign of wealth, because it was so rare.

The room itself was about the size of her classroom at school. More reddish gray flat stones covered the floor.

Shawna stepped out from underneath the balcony, into the open space. To her right, the king sat on his throne, raised up above the floor by a small platform, also built out of wood.

His throne had been built out of shiny black rock. Was it volcanic? Jagged edges stuck up far above his head, while the arms and legs had been polished smooth.

The wall behind the throne held another mosaic. It appeared to be a picture of the palace with the kingdom spread out all around it. The palace itself was outlined with golden bits, while the fields of reeds and water grasses were outlined in black.

Was this part of why the swamp was angry at the king? Was he trying to claim more territory than she'd allowed?

Another…creature talked to the king, so Shawna made her way slowly across the open floor. She guess that the beings standing on the balcony looking down made up the rest of the king's court.

Many of the people there were short and squat, like the guards. The women had beautiful, long dark hair that they wore loose around their heads so it flowed out, all around them, like a mane. The men tended to keep their dark hair cut short. They wore beautiful clothes woven out of reeds and flowers, decorated with shells and gems.

Some of the taller people…were they like her? Dead? Or were they something else? She hoped there might be fairies among them. And maybe a mermaid, too.

The court stood behind a short railing, though Shawna knew that was another human convention—nobody could fall off that balcony. They'd just swim down if they wanted to.

The being talking with the king looked different. More like a fish person, with a great gaping mouth and bulging eyes. She practically had no neck. Her silver skin shone as the scales embedded in it caught the light. A bright purple sash covered her chest. She balanced delicately on her tail, rather than two legs. She had arms, however, they looked more like thick tentacles split at the ends for hands.

Shawna stopped a few feet away from the king and the fish woman, not wanting to overhear what the woman said so urgently to the king. Shawna took her time to look at the king, instead.

He looked like the two guards, short and squat, with a round face and bulging red cheeks. Not regal at all. Shawna swallowed down her disappointment. His nose pointed from his face like a stick, and his chin hung down. He wore a bright yellow and black jacket, puffed up like a honeybee, or maybe like how Shawna looked when she wore her down jacket in the winter. He also wore a grass skirt, though it was a brighter green. At least he had very muscled legs, bulging, with smooth skin. His feet were bare, like Shawna's.

Silver wire made up most of his crown. Bright emeralds, rough diamonds, amethysts, rubies, pearls, and blue-green shells were caught by the swirling loops. It looked both delicate and primitive. It didn't really suit him.

Had he always been king, here? Or had there been someone else, like one of the fish people, who had been king before?

Was this part of the argument with the swamp?

Shawna felt uneasy standing there. She'd always wanted to meet the king. Now, she wasn't so sure.

For all that the silver fish woman looked strange, she appeared, at least to Shawna's eyes, to be much more regal.

Before Shawna could speculate more, the fish person bowed her head and announced loudly enough for the entire court to hear, "This is not the end of this. You will be hearing from us." Then she swam off with dignity, her silvery-scaled skin flashing as she moved.

The king sighed and looked very angry. Shawna remembered when Dad had made such a expression, and Mom had told him to stop it or he'd die of a heart attack.

Then the king shook his head, plastered a smile back on his face and looked directly at Shawna.

"Ah, Rowan, welcome to my kingdom!" he said.

3

Shawna stood, stunned. How could the king mistake her for her twin sister? They'd stopped trying to look identical many, many years before. They never wore the same clothes anymore. Plus, Rowan had cut her hair that spring while Shawna had kept hers long.

Mom had accused them of choosing their hairstyles to be contrary, since Rowan was the more girly one and Shawna was more of a tomboy.

Shawna knew it had just been practical. With her long hair, she could keep it tied back when she went adventuring and exploring. While Rowan could spend time using Mom's hair gel and mousse, getting her shorter hair to style just like her favorite singer's in her latest music video.

"I'm Shawna," she announced to the king. "Not Rowan."

Silence ripped through the court. Though the room had been quiet before, now it seemed very still, poised, as though the water itself had changed from a slow-moving creek to a deep, deceptively calm lake.

The king peered at Shawna. He reached up and stroked his pointed chin with a fat hand. "I see," he finally said after a moment. "No matter. You'll do."

Shawna blinked, surprised. She'd do? She'd do for what? What did the king have planned for her?

Had her death not been an accident? But part of a greater scheme? Had those tricksy reeds been planted there? Acting under his orders?

"Welcome," he said firmly. "I'm glad you're here. Everyone will be so excited to meet you!" He stood up and gestured for her to come closer.

Everyone? Shawna stubbornly stood exactly where she was.

"No one will hurt you," the king said, obviously trying to reassure her. "Not like they can," he added with a chuckle. "You're already dead."

Shawna bristled at that. It didn't seem very polite for him to point out her condition.

Still. What he'd said made sense. She nodded slowly. She didn't have to be afraid of anything now, did she?

Nothing could hurt you once you were dead. Right?

Slowly, Shawna moved forward, walking up the three platform steps to stand beside the king.

He was even shorter than she'd first thought. She could look down on his head, see the thick, dark, wavy hair barely held in place by the weight of the crown. He smelled fishy, too, or maybe that was leftover from the fish woman who'd been standing there earlier.

The king held out his fat hand. Springy black hair stood up between the joints on his fingers, and the backs of his hand had more hair. However, Shawna found it surprisingly soft as she took it, placing the fingers of her hand over the edge of his, like one of the princesses did in the movies she'd watched.

Shawna didn't know what to do next, though it seemed as though the king wanted her to do something. So she tried a curtsey, though it felt awkward and unnatural.

Something Rowan would do, not her.

The king broke into a huge smile. "You'll fit right in," he assured her. Then he turned the pair of them so they were facing out, looking at all the beings up on the balcony. "Come say hello to Shawna," he instructed his court. "Make her feel as welcome as I am."

Some chuckled at that.

Was the king not welcome in his own court? Or did he mean in the swamp?

She gulped as the first of the king's court flowed over the balcony and swam down to meet her, forming a line. It looked like the line that she'd been in when her aunt had gotten married, and everyone coming up to congratulate the happy couple.

The king still held her hand possessively. She found she could still sweat. Gently, she freed it.

The king glared at her for that, but then turned and smiled at the first pair coming up the steps.

Shawna could barely pay attention to their names as she shook their hands. What was the king trying to do? She wasn't about to become his girlfriend or something. Ugh. Not with a short, fat, old man like him.

Would Rowan have accepted an offer from him?

Gladly.

She would have done anything to be a true queen.

Shawna suddenly worried that she wouldn't "do" here in the palace at all.

Shawna looked around the room the king had created for her with distaste. She'd still said *thank you* and had lied about how she'd loved it when he'd showed it to her.

However, it was more and more obvious that the king had been expecting her sister. Anticipating her.

Frilly *girl* stuff filled the room. Pretty pink and blue shells from the long ago ocean covered the walls. Softly waving ferns grew in the corners. There wasn't a bed—evidentially the dead didn't sleep?—but the desk had been carved out of a single piece of white stone with lots of swirls in it. A simple stool woven out of reeds stood before it.

The room even smelled girly, with a faint trace of too-sweet perfume swirling through the water.

A single window had been punched out of the wall, round, and about as big as her head. It did give the room a nice blue tint, but she had to stand on her tiptoes to look out of it, and there wasn't that much to see.

Shawna would have preferred rough shell walls with an interesting texture. Maybe maps of the swamp instead of pretty mosaics.

But what was she supposed to do here? There wasn't anything in the room that interested her.

She really, *really* wanted to explore.

No one had said she had to stay there…

Suddenly, the door burst open. A small being—a child of the same race as the king—came rushing in.

"Quick! You have to hide me!" she pleaded.

She was shorter than the king or the guards, maybe coming up just to Shawna's waist. She was also the only blonde that Shawna had seen—all the others in the court had dark hair. Her round face held that same squished in look, her cheeks pushed out, with a tiny nose and chin. But her face wasn't as red as the others, and her skin seemed darker.

She wore a dress made out of woven yellow reeds. It looked scratchy. It also didn't look as well made as the clothing the court wore.

"Please! Hide me!" The girl looked around the room, frantic.

Shawna couldn't help her shudder. She was too recently dead from playing hide and seek for her to be comfortable hiding anyone. She glanced around the room. Was there a closet?

"There," she said, pointing at the small door against the inner wall. She'd have to duck her head to go into it. It was skinny, too, not much wider than she was.

Then again, she was dead. It wasn't as if she could change clothes. Could she?

"Thank you!" the girl said. She slipped inside quickly.

Shawna closed the door, then went and sat down at the desk, as if writing a letter, though there wasn't anything there for her to write with.

She'd barely composed herself when a frantic knocking startled her.

Before she could even say, "Come in!" the two guards who'd been standing at the door to the court came in.

"How rude!" Shawna told them, pretending to be angry. "You can't just come in here without my permission!"

"Sorry, Miss," the younger guard said, blinking and looking shocked. Did no one talk back to them?

The older guard just growled at her. "Where is she?"

"Where is who?" Shawna asked coldly.

The two guards looked at each other. The younger one shrugged.

"Come on," the older one said, leading the way back out, into the hallway.

The younger one paused as he was closing the door. "You be careful, Miss," he said cautiously.

It looked as though he would have said more, but the other guard called "Come on!" again.

The door shut without a sound. Shawna grinned.

There was much more going on here than a mere game of hide and seek.

When Shawna opened the closet door, she found the little girl sitting on the floor in a ball, her arms wrapped tightly around her knees. "Don't turn me in!" she whispered urgently.

Shawna didn't like the scared look on the girl's face. "I didn't," she said. "And I won't."

The girl blinked at her for a moment, surprised. "Thank you!" she said as she let go of her knees.

The yellow reeds on her dress had bent when she'd been in that awkward position. The ones around her waist now stuck out at odd angles, poking her stomach where they'd folded. The girl stroked her hand over them and smoothed them out.

How had she done that? Reeds didn't just unfold that way.

"Was that magic?" Shawna asked in a hushed voice.

"No," the girl said immediately. "The dress reeds just do that," she added. Then she sighed. "I wish I had a more pretty dress like yours."

Shawna looked down at her white dress. While she kind of liked the ribbons, it wasn't really her style. She'd much rather be wearing shorts or jeans or anything other than a dress.

However, it didn't feel as though she could just take it off. First of all, what would she wear?

But mostly—the dress felt as though it was part of her. She couldn't just remove it. She should be able to change it though. Somehow.

"So what's your name?" Shawna asked. The girl walked out of the closet and stood in the center of the room. She crossed her arms over her chest and looked around, obviously disapproving.

"Kikka," the girl said. "They didn't give you much, did they?"

"No," Shawna said. She felt relieved that she wasn't being ungrateful thinking that the king should have given her more…something. More furniture? A bed? Something to do?

"Why were the guards chasing you? Why don't they like you?" Shawna felt the questions that had been piling up suddenly spill out. "Who is the king? What kind of people are you? Are you at war with the swamp? Or the fish people?"

The girl looked curiously at her. "Are you Rowan?" she asked.

"I'm Shawna," she said, still smarting from the king thinking she was her sister.

The girl's eyes grew wide. "Really?" She suddenly clapped her hand with joy.

The soft sound of her palms hitting together reminded Shawna that they weren't in the air, above the water. Things sounded different here. Smelled different. Felt different.

"That means there's still time," Kikka said.

"For what?" Shawna asked. She still had so many questions, and here was yet one more!

"Revolution."

Kikka grabbed Shawna's hand and tugged her forward. The girl's hand felt warm in Shawna's. Probably the warmest thing she'd felt since she'd died. Kikka was stronger than she looked, too. And possibly older as well. She smelled of warm grass and sunny days, though she looked as though she belonged here, under the water—more than Shawna or the king.

"Come on!" Kikka said. "We've got to escape!"

"What do you mean?" Shawna asked, refusing to move. "And what kind of revolution?" She'd just gotten here! And she'd always wanted to meet the king. Wouldn't it be rude for her to leave so soon?

But she wasn't sure she liked the king. And besides, she'd always said she'd be a great explorer when she grew up…

"We need to get out of the kingdom. Go into the swamp," Kikka said as she looked up and down the hallway outside Shawna's room. "Ask Pantani. She'll know what to do."

Shawna wasn't sure why, but she felt the words, "with you" had been tagged onto the end of that statement.

"Aren't we already in the swamp?" Shawna asked, confused.

Kikka shook her head. "The kingdom is separate. It isn't the same. The king made it so."

Shawna nodded. That made sense to her, thinking about it. She could barely hear the song of the swamp in the palace, as if something blocked it.

Kikka crept down the hallway, looking this way and that.

Shawna walked after her, then stopped at the next door and tried it. It opened into a darker room, but with a large window.

Big enough for the pair of them to swim through.

"This way!" Shawna called to Kikka as she rushed across the room. It looked as though it was a storage space for leftover building supplies: piles of shell pieces filled one corner, while a stack of red bricks lined the wall. In the other corner sat a heap of colored glass pieces—probably used to make the mosaics. A second wall of sturdy white stones stood beside it.

If only she had time to explore everything! She'd spend days going through each and every room.

Shawna didn't see a way to open the window. She pushed hard in the center of the blue glass, then drew her hand back, startled when it easily swung up.

"Out the window!" Shawna told.

"They'll see us!" Kikka complained.

Shawna shrugged. "Maybe. Maybe not. I bet they'll be looking at the doors, watching the trails. Not watching the sky." The king and the guards seemed more human, that way. As if they'd originally been land creatures, not born in the water.

Kikka nodded slowly. "We're not supposed to swim that way," she said slowly.

Now it was Shawna's turn to stare at her. "Why not?"

"That's what the fish people do," Kikka said. "Not the Marikin." At Shawna's puzzled look, she added, "Not us. Not the Orikin either. The king's people."

"But you can still swim?" Shawna asked. Though she was a strong swimmer, she didn't think she was strong enough to carry Kikka with her through the water.

The girl nodded, then grinned. "We can."

"Follow me," Shawna said as she pushed herself off the window ledge and up into the higher water.

It felt wonderfully free to suddenly be swimming. Shawna had always been a good swimmer. It was another one of the things that had made her different than Rowan. Rowan had never liked the water. She's always complained about the coldness of the pool. Rowan took really hot showers when she could, preferring them to baths, not wanting to laze in the hot water.

While Shawna had loved taking baths and cooler showers. She could also float much longer in the water than her twin.

It took a few strokes for Shawna to get up and away from the palace, able to look down. It really did have the shape of a widespread hand, with a tower at the tip of each finger. The base of the palm made up the front of the palace, where she'd come in.

The palace still looked pretty from up here, with its red roofs and white walls.

It also looked completely out of place when she looked at the area surrounding it. Like someone had dropped a building in the middle of a clear field, with no roads leading in or out.

Strange.

Kikka swam up beside her, panting. When she paused, she kept moving her arms and legs. It reminded Shawna of how she'd had to hold herself afloat in the water when she'd been alive.

Why didn't the water just support Kikka? Like it did Shawna?

Suddenly, the guards who'd been chasing Kikka appeared in the courtyard, out behind the palace. They pointed at the pair of them, then rushed back inside.

"We need to run!" Kikka said, obviously frightened.

Dragonflies flashed over their heads, their blue and gold bodies catching what little light there was. Here and gone.

Who would they carry news of their escape to? To the king? Or someone else?

Shawna started swimming away, flowing out, over the back of the palace. It took her a moment to realize that Kikka wasn't beside her.

She paused and looked back. Kikka was trying to swim, but it was obvious she wasn't really a good swimmer. She did something that looked like a dog paddle, but less graceful.

Shawna knew better than to laugh, especially not when the girl looked so scared. She swam back to Kikka, a smooth overhand stroke. "Here," she said. She took the girl's arms and placed them around her neck, so that Kikka floated on her back. Then Shawna took off again, swimming strong and powerfully.

Kikka barely weighed anything at all. Mainly she floated along, her arms warming Shawna's neck.

'Thank you," Kikka whispered in her ear. "You're going so fast!"

Shawna grinned. It was so much more fun to swim like this when she was dead. First of all, she didn't have to worry about breathing, though she turned her head with every other stroke as if she still did. The water didn't push against her as much, though she still pulled herself through it.

The water smelled cleaner up here. And Shawna could hear the song of the swamp again.

The swamp muttered angrily to herself, reminding Shawna of her grandmother when she'd been alive, always arguing with the TV.

"Look out!" Kikka warned.

Shawna instinctively ducked down. Something went whizzing by her head.

Had that been a spear?

She glanced over her shoulder.

The two guards followed after them. They rode what looked like metal seahorses with ugly, bulging red eyes and fangs sticking out of their snouts. The seahorses moved their head and neck forward and back from their body, stiffly, like a kid's toy on a playground.

"We have to go quickly!" Kikka said.

Shawna nodded. Those things looked dangerous. And the guards did, indeed, have at least a dozen spears each that they were throwing at them.

"Where to?" Shawna asked as she dived down, heading straight for the ground.

It didn't work as she thought it ought to—there was no gravity pulling her, making her go faster as she dove. So she leveled out and started swimming up again, as quickly as she could.

"Head left, to the forest of weeds," Kikka said. "Don't stop. Don't look back. Ask to speak with Pantani. She'll listen to you."

Shawna felt Kikka start to let go.

"No!" Shawna said, though she didn't stop swimming. "Where are you going?"

"They'll stop coming after you once they have me," Kikka said. "You need to escape and get help."

"But…"

Before Shawna could stop and catch her, Kikka had fallen from her back.

It appeared that gravity did work on the Marikin, here in the water, as Kikka tumbled slowly toward the ground when she stopped moving, stopped trying to tread water.

Shawna shot upwards again, then stopped and looked back.

The two guards had caught up with Kikka. Each had one of her arms. They didn't look as though they were being gentle with her.

They also appeared to be arguing. One gestured toward Shawna, the other shook his head.

Shawna couldn't breathe a sigh of relief when they turned back. She still felt it all the way from her chest to her belly.

They weren't coming after her. At least, not yet. She figured they would be back, after they carried Kikka to the palace and imprisoned her there.

The guards wouldn't find a trace of Shawna when they came back to this spot, however.

With a powerful kick, Shawna turned away and swam hard, heading toward the dark spot that appeared on the ground to her left, figuring that would be the forest of weeds.

She just hoped that Pantani would be able to help her rescue Kikka. Because that was what Shawna had to do next.

4

Thick wavy weeds reached up toward the air. Shawna didn't think she'd be able to swim over the tops of them, though she kind of wanted to. The leaves grew wide, maybe two feet across, though they were thin, not much thicker than paper. The water here had grown murky, so the weeds appeared a dark green color.

She must be so small now! For the weeds to be so big.

Shawna swam back down to the ground. She was surprised at how long it took her. Was the swamp actually that deep? Or had she shrunk down as well? She patted her face, but it didn't feel squished in.

A thick, spicy scent flowed from the weeds. It was kind of like the smell of pine trees, though it was a deeper scent, tickling the back of her throat. She shivered, the water here much cooler.

Mud covered the ground instead of nice sand or gravel. It squelched between her toes. Ugh.

Could she walk above the ground? Maybe float and just push her way along? She pushed herself forward, into the weeds. They grew too closely together for her to be able to properly swim. She could pull herself along, grabbing onto one, then the next. But the weeds, too, felt slimy, and covered her fingers with a green goo.

How could she get her hands clean? She stopped just inside the weed forest, planting her feet solidly on the mud and rubbed her hands together.

That got off most of the muck. She looked over her shoulder. The weeds had moved back into place, so she couldn't see past the end of them and out into the clearer water.

If Shawna's heart still beat, she knew she'd feel it pounding with fear. She couldn't take a deep breath to calm herself. She rolled her shoulders instead and took a deep gulp of…whatever it was she was gulping. Not water, but not air either.

She could do this. What could hurt her here, anyway? She was already dead.

Bravely, Shawna turned forward again. Besides, this was a forest for her to explore. She told herself to be excited. Despite the yucky mud. The slimy green stems of the weeds. The way she had to blink her eyes to clear them from the hazy water. The thick smell that threatened to choke her.

Shawna walked forward for a while. Or at least she thought she was moving forward. She hadn't walked out of the weed woods yet. Hopefully she wasn't walking in circles, though she didn't know where she was going.

Pantani lived here? Where? Shawna didn't see any trails.

She stopped. If she called out, would the guards hear her?

She doubted they'd be coming after her here, in this woods. She bet they didn't like it any more than she did.

Plus, she heard the swamp all around her here. Muttering. Angry. She would say frightening, but she wasn't going to be scared.

"Pantani?" Shawna called. Her voice still sounded weak with no air behind it. "Pantani!" She tried to shout, though to her ears it still was no more than a whisper. "Kikka sent me," she added. "I need your help."

The swamp paused in her muttering.

Though Shawna couldn't breathe, she felt as though the swamp could. And did. And that it had just taken a deep breath.

Slowly, the weeds directly in front of Shawna started to wave. They moved from side to side, then slid apart, making a path for her to follow.

Shawna gulped. She wasn't scared (she wasn't!). She was also excited.

She marched forward, between the weeds, off to her next adventure.

The darkness of the weed forest bothered Shawna. She wished for her little lights, the ones that had marked the borders of the swamp.

But there was no border here. She was deep in the heart of the swamp. These weeds didn't mark the swamp's territory: they filled it. The smell had changed—instead of spicy, it now smelled more like dry grass. Which impressed Shawna, given how far under the water she'd walked.

Green stains marred her pretty white dress. She told herself she didn't care—she hadn't liked it that much anyway. She hoped she would be able to clean it, though, once she left the woods. Her feet, too, carried the muck she walked through. She'd haphazardly braided her hair but it wouldn't stay knotted.

Hopefully Pantani wouldn't mind her being so dirty. Or would at least understand.

The song of the swamp filled Shawna's ears, so loud she couldn't make out the words or feelings anymore. It just sounded like noise. She hoped it wouldn't get much louder, or she would find out if her ears could hurt even though she was dead.

Finally, Shawna saw a light ahead of her. She hurried forward.

The mud grew thicker. Shawna slowed down when she saw how much gunk she kicked into the water.

At least whoever was waiting for her would know she was coming. The air felt more humid, the water heavier, somehow. Despite that, Shawna still shivered.

The light gave way to an opening. Shawna eagerly stepped into it, looking around.

Disappointment struck her. There wasn't much to see. Just an open area in the weeds. Tiny blobs of light floated above her head, like a collection of slow-moving fireflies.

"Pantani?" Shawna called.

The weeds directly across from her shivered.

An old woman walked out.

Well, she was kind of like a woman.

She had reeds sprouting out of the top of her head, the cattails forming a crown. Stringy, dark green weeds hung down beneath them, like greasy hair. Her eyes looked like rotting walnuts, all shriveled, set deeply into her face. Her nose stuck out, oddly shaped, like a badly carved potato. She grinned at Shawna with her overly large mouth, the lips flabby and painted a bright red.

Dark brown sack-like material covered the rest of her lumpy body. It reminded Shawna of a scarecrow, badly stuffed with straw. The dress covered her arms, with gnarled hands sticking out of the ends. The skirt flowed down and dragged on the mud, the hem covered in it.

The old woman had a stick in one hand, a gnarled piece of ancient wood. The top of it held a huge black pearl, the size of Shawna's two fists held together. It cast an oddly dark light.

When the woman opened her mouth, song poured out.

Shawna blinked, surprised. How could such an old, pieced-together creature make such a beautiful sound?

The melody lifted Shawna's heart. She felt herself smiling. She bobbed her head in time with the gentle beat.

Something floated up, catching Shawna's eye. She realized that the dirt and slime were lifting from her dress, freed by the song. The rest of the water in the open area cleared as well.

When the woman finished, Shawna clapped her hands, the hollow, quiet noise still sounding loud after the song.

"Are you Pantani?" Shawna asked.

The woman shrugged.

"Who are you?" Shawna asked. The woman could speak, right? She'd just sung a song!

The old woman waved her tall staff, making the weeds around them dance for a moment, as if that answered Shawna's question.

"I'm Shawna," she said, moving forward.

The old woman nodded impatiently, as if she already knew that.

"I need help. I need to go rescue Kikka," Shawna told the woman. "She told me to find Pantani, here in the weed forest."

The woman sang a brief song. It reminded Shawna of a robin's early morning song.

But she didn't hear any words in it.

"Why won't you answer me?" Shawna asked, frustrated. Who was this woman? Why was she here? Why wouldn't she help?

The woman sighed and held out her hand. Before she let Shawna take it, though, she sang a mournful tune.

This time Shawna understood.

Something would happen to Shawna if she took the old woman's hand. Something that would make Shawna sad.

"Can you help?" Shawna asked the woman directly.

Slowly, the woman nodded.

Could Shawna only understand the woman's song if she held onto her hand? She didn't know what was going on. She desperately wanted to learn, though.

"Rowan…"

The word sighed through the water.

"I'm not Rowan!" Shawna said indignantly.

The woman nodded impatiently. She knew that.

The name floated through the water again. "Rowan…"

Why was her sister important?

Then she remembered that the king had been expecting her sister. Had been prepared for her. He'd said that Shawna "would do".

But Shawna had escaped. She would bet that she wouldn't "do" now.

Did the king have plans for Rowan? Did he want to kill her too? Make both sisters dead?

Shawna took another step toward the old woman. "If I take your hand, can you help Rowan too?"

The old woman stared hard at Shawna, her black, wrinkled eyes showing no mercy, no promise.

It wasn't up to the old woman to save Rowan. Only Shawna could do that.

"All right," Shawna said. "I'll do it."

She wasn't sure what exactly she was agreeing to. She told herself that it couldn't be too bad. She was already dead, right?

A little voice inside her head told her she was lying.

The old woman's hand felt bony and hard in Shawna's, like a bag with thick sticks. The smell of the swamp, what Shawna remembered from when she'd been alive, dried grasses and the mustiness of cattails, washed over her. A thrill of excitement spiked through her, making her very warm suddenly.

At the same time, Shawna fought to keep her eyes open. She wanted to *see*. For a moment she nearly pulled back, panicked. This felt too much like dying, when she'd been forced to rest.

Blinking furiously, she watched the old woman change. She lost her human form, her bulk fanning out until she looked more like a blob. Her head still had its crown of cattails and her hair still looked like greasy weeds.

But the old woman now floated in front of her, like a matt of grass that kept shifting and changing shape. The "hand" Shawna held onto was just the branch of a spindly tree. Bright lights swam around and through the creature. Tufts of grass sprang up, and deep moss. She smelled of water and weeds.

However, the shape of the creature looked familiar. With the one staff sticking straight up, and the rest floating around it like a crooked continent.

With a gasp, Shawna realized what she was looking at.

The swamp.

She'd seen the plans Dad had laid out when he'd wanted to drain the waters away. The form of the being in front of her matched the outline of the swamp exactly.

The part that Shawna had always thought of as a fist pushing into the orchard was the creature's great staff.

"You're the swamp!" Shawna exclaimed.

Why did her voice suddenly sound so much louder? As if she had air in her lungs?

A chuckle greeted her. "Yes, I am. The Orikin know me as Pantani, the old one."

"Who are the Orikin? And the Marikin? How did they get here? Who is the king? Why does he want Rowan?" Shawna knew she wasn't giving Pantani a chance to answer any of her questions, but they'd built up so much!

"I don't have time to tell you everything," Pantani replied.

"Why not?" Shawna asked, not hiding her frustration though she knew her mother would fuss at her for sounding like a two year old.

Pantani gestured with her staff toward Shawna's feet.

Shawna gasped. Black veins now stood up out of the white skin on the tops of her feet.

"By touching you, really touching you, I've made you a part of me," Pantani said. "I'm sorry."

"What does that mean?" Shawna asked. She tried to let go of the creature's hand but found herself roughly held.

"It means you only have a short time left, as yourself," Pantani admitted. "In a while, you'll become part of me."

Shawna shivered. She didn't like the sounds of that. "I won't be me anymore?" she asked, trying to understand.

"You will no longer be separate from me," Pantani said. "You'll stop thinking and acting on your own. That's what happens to all creatures who come down here to live. They become part of me, part of the swamp. Or they die."

Shawna found she could still take that big gulp to swallow down her fear. "And since I'm already dead…"

"You'll just cease to be." Pantani shrugged. "It's my way. The way of nature."

Shawna found that even though she was dead, tears could still form in her eyes. "So I'll die die. Really dead die."

"Yes," Pantani said.

"I need to save my sister before then," Shawna said bravely pushing away her own sadness. She didn't want to truly die.

But it was better that, then Rowan. Mom and Dad wouldn't survive the pair of them dying.

"Yes," Pantani said. She sounded grateful. "Before the king takes her too."

"Why don't the Orikin change and become part of you?" Shawna asked.

"Because of the king," Pantani said, scowling. "They once lived above the water, outside the swamp. They took care of the orchard. Blessed the blossoms when they first bloomed, sipped dew from the leaves, polished the apples as they grew."

"Like fairies?" Shawna asked. They sure sounded like some sort of tiny magical creature. And that would explain their red cheeks and scrunched in faces. She'd seen dolls made from dried apples.

The king and the guards looked exactly like that.

Pantani nodded slowly. She squeezed Shawna's hand and sang a trill of music.

Shawna *saw* what the Orikin used to be, how they used to live. They looked older out of the water, and they wore grass and leaves instead of reeds. But they still moved the same, with their squat little legs.

They *belonged* on the land. Not in the water. They didn't have the grace of the fish people.

"And Kikka isn't an Orikin? But a Marikin?" Shawna asked when she noticed that all the fairies she saw had black or brown hair.

"They're very similar," Pantani said. "But her people tended the reeds. They lived on the shores of the swamp."

Again, after a short burst of song, Shawna saw people who looked more like Kikka, with blonde hair. They had tiny boats that they used for moving among the reeds. She watched them all stop and stand in their boats, raising their hands as they welcomed the coming sun. Their houses were on the land, though, built of straw and reeds.

"Why are they here? The Marikin and the Orikin?" Shawna asked. "They don't belong here. Not any of them."

Pantani sighed. "The Orikin wanted more land for their trees. They couldn't just take it, though, from the Marikin, who protect the border."

Shawna realized that the Marikin were the ones who lit the lights that marked the border between swamp and land. That yellowish-brown light.

"So the Orikin moved here, to change the nature of the swamp. To claim it for the land," Pantani said. "But they couldn't just take over."

Shawna remembered that stand of trees that she'd found as she'd walked toward the king's palace. Had that been their first attempt? Had the trees died instead of growing?

"The Orikin need to strengthen their ties with the land. And for that, they need Rowan," Pantani said.

"And they got the wrong sister," Shawna said, nodding. "But how would that work?"

"She is the true heir of the orchard," Pantani said. "Through her blood, the Orikin could bring the land here."

"The swamp's protected," Shawna protested. "It's been declared a wetlands. Dad can't drain it."

"Pfttt," Pantani said. She made a noise like wind blowing through dry reeds. "That's a human thing. What would your father do if the water suddenly just drained away, on its own?"

Shawna nodded. "Probably plant more trees." She looked out, back at the weed forest. It was a truly alien place. The waving leaves didn't look human at all.

And it would all be lost. And her sister, too.

"How do I stop them?" Shawna asked.

"You need to destroy the castle," Pantani said. "I let them build it here, believing that they could do no harm."

"How do I do that?" Shawna asked.

"If I knew that, I already would have," Pantani replied sharply. Then she sighed, sounding like pine needles rustling.

That deep rich smell of bay leaves washed over Shawna. "Kikka had a plan that involved the fish attacking the castle. But then she was captured."

"I need to rescue Kikka," Shawna said. Which was good, because she'd already planned on doing that.

"You might rescue the rest of her people, first," Pantani said. "They're trapped at the edges of the land, caught up in their own reeds."

Shawna blinked. It sounded like there were so many things to set to right down here! And she didn't know how long she had, how long she would be able to act on her own, before she became part of the swamp, part of Pantani.

"I will send you to Zilba. She will be able to help," Pantani said.

"But—" Shawna still had so many questions! And she needed a plan. Just storming the castle didn't seem like a good idea.

The hard hand that held hers melted away. Weeds sprang up, waving directly in front of her face, blocking her view. Shawna found herself floating along on a hard current, blowing her back and away.

She almost wished she could curse like Dad did when he was really angry. But she'd tried not to listen to him when he got that way.

Instead, she swam along the current, trusting that it would take her where she needed to go.

The swamp—Pantani—needed her help. So did Kikka and the rest.

And Pantani had been right. Rowan was much more a daughter of the orchard. It was Shawna who'd always loved the swamp, had always dreamed of exploring it.

Maybe the reeds had drowned the right sister after all.

5

The coldness of the water made Shawna shiver as she swam along. She didn't like the dim murkiness of it either. It reminded her why she hadn't wanted to go into the swamp in the first place. The slime that covered the top of it. The mud. How it stank.

Still, this was the direction that Pantani had sent her in, so Shawna swam deeper.

A silver flash startled her.

It was one of the fish people. "What are you doing here?" the woman demanded. Was it the same woman Shawna had seen at the court? She seemed more fishlike now. She still wore a purple sash but it was pinned in place under a couple of scales. She had no neck flowing from her head to her body. Her mouth still gaped and her eyes had grown big and bulbous.

"Pantani sent me," Shawna said. Her voice still sounded louder than it had, before. Was it because she spoke with more of the voice of the swamp? "I'm looking for Zilba."

"I am Zilba," the woman said, nodding. "I saw you at the court."

"Yes!" Shawna said, excited that this was the same woman.

"What happened to you?" Zilba asked. She quickly swam a circle around Shawna, opening and closing her mouth several times, as if tasting the water around her.

"I escaped," Shawna said. "With the help of Kikka. But they recaptured her."

"The Orikin have captured much of the Merikin," Zilba said sadly. "Trapped them in reeds."

"How do we rescue them?" Shawna asked. Wasn't that what Pantani needed for her to do? While she could still move and be separate?

Zilba blinked her big eyes at Shawna. "Rescue them? Why would we do that?"

Shawna contained her sigh. She'd always thought the fish living in the swamp were kind of stupid. She'd hoped she'd been wrong.

"So that we can go and rescue Kikka and destroy the palace together!" Shawna exclaimed.

Zilba bobbed her head up and down, which made her whole body see-saw as well. "We don't like the palace," she said slowly.

"That's right," Shawna said. "We don't like the palace."

"They change the water," Zilba said, anger dripping into her tone. "They make it clear."

Shawna shrugged. She'd actually enjoyed the clearer water near the palace. This water felt too closed in to her. And cold. And kind of slimy, if she was being honest.

"They take away our food," Zilba said. "The plants can't grow in the clear water."

"Then we have to stop them," Shawna said firmly.

Zilba shook her head. Again, it caused her whole body to move. "The king said he would stop."

"The king lies," Shawna told the fish woman. "He wants to take over the whole swamp. Drain the water. Make more land. More orchard."

"We need the water," Zilba said. "We have already given up territory to the king."

"We need to stop the king," Shawna said.

"How?" Zilba finally asked.

"We need to rescue the Merikin. They know how," Shawna said firmly. She knew she was stretching the truth. But hopefully not too much.

If Kikka had had a plan, maybe she'd told someone about it.

"So by rescuing the Merikin, we can stop the king?" Zilba asked.

"Yes," Shawna said firmly.

Zilba swam another quick circle around Shawna. "Stay here," she said. "I will gather my kin."

Then she swam off, into the dim water. Shawna quickly lost track of where she was.

Should she stay here? Should she follow? Would the fish woman even remember why she was going to get her kin?

Before Shawna could start swimming after her, Zilba returned. "Catch hold of my fin," she instructed Shawna. "And hold on."

Shawna swam up and over the great silver fish. Zilba wasn't that much larger than Shawna, only by a head or so.

Shawna reached over Zilba's back and held onto a fin with each hand.

Suddenly, Shawna found herself singing a trilling note, like a hunter's charge.

When she finished, she shook herself. She hadn't known that song. It had just come out of her. Like one of the songs of the swamp.

She glanced down at her feet. The black lines had just crossed her ankles.

She was becoming more like the swamp.

She was still determined to do everything she needed to do first: rescue Kikka, destroy the palace, save her sister.

Before all her words turned into song.

The water wasn't much clearer near the edges of the swamp, where the water met the land. It was, however, much brighter. Shawna could see the muck floating in it.

But she also watched Zilba's people dart up and suck down some of that muck as they swam along. It was their food.

It made Shawna really angry that the king was taking away the fish people's food. Even if they weren't that smart. Though they were much smarter with a group of them together than Zilba had been on her own.

They stopped a few feet away from the reeds. The water was much clearer here.

Two Orikin guards stood in front of the reeds. It wasn't the same pair that Shawna had seen before. They were both older, looking wizened, as if they'd spent a lot of time in the sun.

They had spears, though, as well as their swords. They wore cattail suspenders over woven grass skirts.

They stood on the rocky ground of the swamp floor, in front of the abrupt edge leading up to the surface. Behind them, tall yellow reeds grew up, out of the side of the dirt. The reeds were each as big around as Shawna, growing so tightly together that she couldn't have squeezed through them.

Shawna caught a glimpse of yellow hair peeking out at them from behind the reeds, then disappearing again.

This was where Kikka's people were being held.

A frantic hand waved at Shawna from the far right side of the patch of reeds. A head popped out, then back in.

Could the Merikin escape that way? Climb out of their cage?

All that Shawna and the fish people had to do was to create a distraction, then.

"Go to the left," Shawna instructed Zilba. "Then circle back to the right. Make the guards face away from the far end of the cage."

The soft movement of Zilba's entire body as she nodded made Shawna grin. It was so much fun riding a fish!

Maybe even after she became part of the swamp, she'd still be able to do that. Enjoy catching a ride on the back of Zilba or the others.

Zilba circled slowly then swam out of the dim water, approaching the clearer water cautiously.

She changed as she did, becoming more like a person, less like a fish.

Shawna slid from Zilba's back and walked beside her, still holding onto one of her fins.

Was that part of what the Orikin did when they changed the water? Made it so only people-like creatures could live there?

"What are you doing here?" Shawna asked the guards as they came swimming up. "The palace is under attack!"

"What?" the guards asked, looking surprised.

"Quickly, you must go back! Save the poor king!" Shawna said, pouring it on.

Her mom had always called her a good little actress.

"But how?" the guard on the left asked.

"And who?" asked the guard on the right.

"Starfish people," Shawna confided in them. "They look like starfish. They've crept here from the other waters and want to take over!"

She hoped that the guards even out here understood the king's plans. And that they'd mistake her for Rowan as well. That they wouldn't know she wasn't her sister. She was still wearing that white dress, after all.

Behind the guards, she saw one of the Orikin slip out from between the bars of reeds. Then another.

"Why did the king send you?" the guard on the left asked, looking shrewdly at her.

"He sent me away to keep me safe," Shawna said, maintaining her innocence. "You must protect me! And save the king!"

The one on the left nodded. "We can do that. Just come—"

Both of the guards turned as one.

"Stop! They're escaping!" the one guard called.

Shawna grabbed hold of the guard closest to her so he couldn't draw his sword. "You have to let them go," she said sternly. "It isn't right to imprison them!"

The other guard looked back at her in horror. "It's a trick!" he said loudly.

"Help me!" Shawna called out. She gave a trilling song— something from the swamp.

As one, Zilba's people came swimming up. They crowded around the guards, pushing them this way and that, nibbling at their arms and legs and heads.

The guards didn't know which way to turn. They were being attacked from all sides. Shawna kept hold of the arm of the one guard. He kept trying to pull out of her grip but she held on.

More of the Merikin escaped, streaming out from their prison of reeds.

"Just wait until the king hears of this," the guard told Shawna darkly.

She shrugged. She didn't particularly like the king anymore.

Had she been the one who'd first come up with stories about him? Or had it been Rowan? She didn't remember who'd first started talking about him.

It didn't matter.

He wouldn't be in the swamp for long. Not if Shawna had her say.

After the last of the Merikin left their prison, Zilba's people started pressing the guards back. It took Shawna a moment to realize that they were intending to imprison the guards there now.

"Wait!" Shawna called. It wasn't right to imprison anyone.

"It will be all right," Zilba said, sliding up to Shawna. "It's just for a little while. We want to get to the palace first."

Shawna nodded slowly. She still didn't like it, but she could see why Zilba wanted to hold them.

"Just for a short while?" Shawna asked as the guards finally stepped back and through the reeds.

Zilba opened and closed her gaping mouth a couple of times.

Was she laughing?

"My people won't stay here guarding for very long," she said after a moment. "Just long enough."

"So now…we go back to the palace?" Shawna guessed as she climbed onto Zilba's back.

"To rescue Kikka. Yes," Zilba said as she sped off.

Though Shawna couldn't breathe, she still found that her equivalent of "breathing" easier once they left the cleaner water around the reeds. She never would have thought she'd welcome the dimmer, murkier water of the rest of the swamp.

Pantani's song burst from her again, a song of happiness and welcome. It reminded her of spring, of the dripping sounds of snow melting. Or warmer days and frost filled nights. Of the first crocus pushing up above the ground, the first new reeds.

Shawna *felt* the spring deeply as she sang. It wasn't something she merely watched: the season now lived within her, deep in her bones, stirring her blood as the days grew warmer.

Was this what it meant to be part of the swamp? To experience the seasons, live them completely?

Shawna had to admit it made her curious. It was a new thing to explore.

Maybe becoming part of Pantani didn't mean giving up all of her exploring days.

Shawna loved how fast Zilba swam through the swamp. It felt like flying.

Merikin rode on the backs of the fish. Shawna remembered that Kikka hadn't been able to swim very much or very far. Gravity worked on her kind here in the swamp. Sort of. While Shawna felt light as a feather. She knew if she didn't hold on tightly to Zilba's fin, she'd fly off and away.

She was almost tempted to do just that, at least once, just to see what it felt like.

More than one of the Merikin came swimming up close to Shawna. They reached out and patted Zilba, or touched her leg. One of the smaller, younger ones actually stroked her hair.

Shawna realized they were saying thank you for rescuing them.

Now, together, they were going to rescue Kikka. Was she a princess? A queen? And how were they going to do it?

The king didn't have many guards, at least not that Shawna had seen. But he did have a lot of people in the court. Some of whom hadn't been Orikin. She'd hoped they were fairies or elves or something.

Now, she hoped they were cowards.

The great school of fish and swarm of Merikin gathered at the edge of the clear water, looking out on the palace. It still looked pretty to Shawna, with its white stone walls, the blue ferns, the red rocks around the doors and windows.

It also looked out of place. That much she could tell, now. It was too clean to be of the swamp, the lines too hard and unnatural. It had made her human-self feel more comfortable.

But the side of her that was slowly becoming part of the swamp despised it with a deep, abiding hatred. The strength of that feeling surprised Shawna.

How were they to attack it, though? The fish couldn't just swim up and start nipping at the walls. That would take too much time. Plus, the guards had spears. And sharp swords crossed on their backs that she knew they won't hesitate to use, cutting up the fish people.

She looked around.

The king had changed the floor of the swamp here. Instead of the natural mud, he'd covered it with gravel and sand.

Could they use that?

Shawna picked up one of the bigger rocks. It felt light in her hands. When she let go of it in mid-air, it plopped promptly back down on the ground again.

She picked the rock up again and heaved it. It flew a surprising long way, landing close to the front door of the palace.

It gave her an idea.

She turned to Zilba. "Have you ever heard of baseball?"

It didn't take long for Shawna and the Merikin to gather up a large quantity of stones and boulders. Shawna wasn't sure how they'd heave the bigger rocks, but Zilba assured her that they could.

Shawna took one last look at the palace. It was a pretty sight.

But it couldn't stay here.

At her signal, three of the Merikin tossed large rocks up in front of them.

A moment later, all three went sailing through the water. Zilba's people had struck each one with a massive fish tail, like a bat.

Two missed.

But the third landed squarely on the cone-shaped red rooftop of the closest tower and crushed it.

Shawna couldn't help but feel disappointed that there wasn't a resounding *crash* when it struck. She didn't know if she'd ever get used to how all the sound was muted under the water.

She'd just have to remember to stick her head up above the water sometimes and listen to the birds sing.

The Merikin and the fish people developed better accuracy: All the rocks struck hard in the next volley. And the next.

Chunks of the closest tower broke away. A gaping hole appeared in the front wall. Windows smashed and Shawna thought she heard the faint tinkling of glass.

Guards rushed out, only to be driven back inside by the next cascade of rocks.

Shawna counted them as quickly as she could—there had been at least a dozen. Probably more.

One of the Merikin claimed that they'd found Kikka. The small fish had agreed to spy for them. She was being held in the back part of the palace. The Orikin had never dug underground, so she wasn't in a dungeon or something.

The Merikin had already divided themselves into groups: a chain of reed people supplying more rocks, rock tossers for the fish people, and a third group that readied themselves to protect the first two. They didn't have swords, but they held sharp knives made of thorns.

Shawna and Zilba left the others to continue their attack. As quickly as they could, they swam around to the far side of the palace.

Large groups of the Orikin had gathered in the gardens back there, between the towers. They squealed or shuddered when a hit came too close. They seemed lost, unsure of what to do.

Shawna felt bad. She was destroying their home.

Then again, if she didn't stop them, they'd destroy hers.

No guards stood back here. She figured they were all up front, getting ready to attack.

Which meant Shawna could go rescue Kikka.

But where was the Merikin being held?

Shawna made Zilba swim along the length of the palace, looking for a blonde head. Or a red flag. Or something.

She didn't see anything.

Zilba considered. "Fish swim in holes," she said finally. "Look for the holes."

What did that mean?

Shawna wasn't certain that Zilba would make much sense away from the rest of her people. It was as though when they were together, as a group, they were much smarter.

"Okay," Shawna said as they swam along the edge of the palace one more time.

Instead of looking at where the Orikin were gathered together, she paid attention to the spaces they avoided. Where they didn't stand.

There. On the side of the fourth tower. They seemed to avoid that spot. Why?

Was the water bad there? It didn't look any less clear.

But there was something the Orikin didn't like about that area.

Kikka had to be kept in that tower. Shawna would bet up on the second story, where there were no windows.

How could they get into, though? They couldn't approach it and not be seen. Would the Orikin try to stop them, however? They seemed very confused right now.

A lucky shot hit the roof of the fourth tower, smashing it. The people below shrieked and scurried away.

Shawna would have laughed at how they scuttled, kind of like crabs. But that would have been mean, and she did try not to be mean.

Instead, she urged Zilba up, directly toward the now broken-in roof.

She ignored the Orikin who pointed and shouted at her. Ignored it when a couple of brave souls also threw rocks that bounced off her leg.

Would they come swimming up to get her? Maybe. They were that angry.

"Go," Shawna told Zilba as she slipped off the fish's back. "Stay safe."

Zilba shook her head violently, making her whole body shake back and forth. "I stay with you."

"The hole's too small for you," Shawna pointed out. "You can't fit. And the tower isn't made for your people, either. Go back to the edges and watch for my signal."

"What signal?" Zilba asked.

Shawna tried to do a warbling song of the swamp. She really did. She put all her fear into it.

No sound came out, though. The king had dampened all of Pantani's influence.

If Shawna stayed in the clean water of the Orikin, would it slow her change? Would she be able to stay separate from the swamp?

No. The king still wanted to kill her sister. Shawna had to stop him, no matter the cost to herself.

"I will wait and watch," Zilba told Shawna. The fish woman lifted off the roof and swam away.

A group of the Orikin swam after her.

Shawna shivered. Hopefully Zilba would be able to take care of herself. She could swim much faster than any of the Orikin.

Shawna would just have to plan on getting away herself.

She gulped when she realized that a few of the Orikin were now struggling to swim upward toward her.

Time to get a rescuing.

Shawna couldn't help but giggle as she pulled herself through the hole in the roof.

Maybe she'd have to make up a song about that someday, to sing in the voice of the swamp.

If she could remember enough of herself to do so.

6

The top part of the tower hadn't been cleaned in a while. If it had been up above the swamp, it probably would have been filled with spiderwebs and dust. As it was, little fish had crept in, no longer than her thumb, and made their homes here. Soft weeds grew between the cracks in the stone floor.

Whoomp!

Shawna jumped, startled. Then she had to laugh at herself. She shouldn't just stand there, not when the palace was under attack. She might find herself trapped under a boulder.

A winding passage led down from the top room of the tower. It didn't actually have stairs, but rails on either side that Shawna pulled herself along. It was yet another human thing. Why not just have a single pole and swim up and down from the top level to the bottom?

Rough rock made up the walls, as if it had been carved in a hurry. It wasn't decorated or pretty, not like the rest of the palace. Shawna actually liked it more.

The hallway went along the outside wall of the round tower, with a solid cone at the center. She found it was easier to pull herself along rather than to swim, so she hauled herself down the winding passage, one hand at a time, skimming as fast as she could.

"Kikka!" Shawna called out, certain that her guards had already left. "Kikka!"

Down two levels, Shawna finally heard a weak voice call out, "Here!"

Shawna found a closed stone door. Iron straps ran across the top and the bottom of it, like an old-fashioned gate. A huge padlock hung from the handle. It was as big as Shawna's head. She could fit three fingers into the keyhole.

No window in the door let her look in.

"Kikka?" Shawna called as she pounded on the door. "It's me. Shawna. We're here to rescue you!"

"Shawna?" Kikka asked. "Yes, I remember. You should have just let me be. Not risked yourself."

"Have you heard the thumps?" Shawna asked as she tugged at the lock. She didn't like how defeated Kikka sounded. "Those are rocks being used to tear down the palace."

"Really?" The voice sounded stronger, as if Kikka was just waking up. "How are you doing that?"

"We rescued the Merikin," Shawna told her. How the heck was she supposed to get Kikka out? The door was solid. As were the walls. "And Zilba and the fish people came with me to attack the palace."

"They won't work together for very long," Kikka warned.

"Why not?" Shawna asked. They were winning! The palace was being knocked to bits. Why would they just stop?

Because they won't remember," Kikka said with a sigh. "Remembering…that's much more of a human thing."

"Were you touched by Pantani?" Shawna asked.

The gasp from behind the door must have been really loud for Shawna to still have heard it. "I wasn't. I was touched by you. But you were touched by the swamp, weren't you?"

"I was," Shawna said. She couldn't cry, now that she was dead. She still found she had a lump in her throat. She felt sad for all the things she would lose, despite how much she loved the swamp.

She glanced down. The black veins still crept up her legs. They hadn't reached her knees yet, but it was just a matter of time.

"Can you sing the door down?" Kikka asked.

Sing? Shawna wished she could take a deep breath and sigh. "The Orikin change the water," she complained. "It's hard to hear the swamp here."

"I know," Kikka said. Her voice took on its own sing-song tones. "But you must try, my dear. Try and try!"

Shawna heard the overtones of Pantani in Kikka's voice. Could she reach out to the old woman here?

She moved her hand from the door (that obviously, the Okrikin had made) and touched the rough stone instead. That was more natural. It came from deep under the swamp itself, the land the swamp rested on.

The burbling sound that rolled out of Shawna's mouth surprised her. It almost sounded like a song that Zilba would sing, popping air bubbles with her big, gaping mouth. The song trilled up, going much higher in pitch than Shawna could when she'd been alive, not without screeching.

The song dirtied the water. Mud and soft green weeds oozed from the rock walls. Ferns sprang up. The tiny fish Shawna had seen at the top of the tower suddenly swam down and around her, feeding on the newly sprouted reeds.

"Keep going!" Kikka called.

Though had Kikka said that with her voice? Shawna wasn't sure. She'd felt more than heard the words, as though they'd been taped into her bones directly.

Or maybe it hadn't been Kikka who'd spoken.

Shawna continued to sing of the land surrounding the swamp. It wasn't that Pantani hated it. She just jealously guarded her borders so the land didn't try to take more from her.

Shawna colored the song, herself. The Orikin were from the land. The orchard. The bright spring blossoms, the droning of bees, the tartness of the first apples before the frost had kissed them, sweetened them. The feel of dry grass in the heat of the summer, the rustling of leaves in the fall.

The memories of the orchard passed from Shawna as she put them into the song. They flowed out like the tears she wanted to cry, all the sweetness of home and the trees, the endless blue sky, the way the stars danced at night.

When Shawna came back to herself, she realized she floated high in the air.

The tower had dissolved itself around her, gone back to the swamp.

Looking down, Shawna saw more of the results of her song. The stones tumbling out of their unnatural alignment, falling back into random patterns. Fish swam happily between the growing weeds and ferns. Mud filled the bottom of the swamp, rich with food for the life that was supposed to live there.

"You did it!" Kikka said.

Shawna nodded. She felt the loss of where all her love of the orchard had been. She turned to the Merikin, and gasped.

Kikka had aged in the prison. Her bright yellow hair had turned gray. Wrinkles creased her squat face. Her hand shook, the knuckles swollen.

"What happened?" Shawna asked, horrified.

"We do not belong under the water," Kikka said, her voice gentle. "We need the sun. Being trapped with no light…" She shrugged.

"If you go spend time in the sunshine, will you change back?" Shawna asked. She reached out her hand to squeeze the old woman's. The skin felt soft, worn with age, though the bones were still strong.

"Maybe," Kikka said. She winked at Shawna. "There might be some strength left in this old body. But come. You must meet the king."

Shawna bit her lips together. She didn't want to go back and see the king. She'd destroyed his palace. Maybe even killed some of his people.

"He wants to say goodbye," Kikka told her. "You should let him."

Shawna sighed but nodded. She'd go see the king.

She checked her legs. The black veins had reached far above her knees. She pressed her hand against her hip. She felt the warmth of the swamp under her fingertips there, but not above her waist.

She had time. Then she needed to do one last thing before she lost herself in Pantani.

Shawna couldn't help but be glad at how old and wizened the king looked. She knew it was mean. She didn't care. He'd made Kikka that old. He should feel that age, too.

His jacket still looked fuzzy, made out of black fur like a bumblebee's. The grass skirt he wore had dark stains—Shawna hoped it wasn't blood. The cattails he'd worn as suspenders had broken and tufts of fur haloed out from the ends.

He didn't scowl or look angry with her, though his first words were, "You changed our plans."

"They were bad plans," Shawna told him.

The king shook his head from side to side, not agreeing or disagreeing. "You did remind us of up top, what it's like to live in the orchard."

Shawna nodded and took a gulping swallow instead of a deep breath. Or possibly crying. She remembered the orchard, still, but not as well. It was almost as though living there had happened to someone else. It felt distant. Her heart ached, but dully.

"I have to thank you for that," the king said. His voice sounded kind, even if his eyes still bore angry holes through her. "It will make it easier to leave."

"And you'll stay up top, in the orchard, where you belong," Shawna told him.

Though she wasn't singing, she found that she was using the voice of the swamp.

"We will," the king said. Then he added slyly, "For now, at any rate."

Shawna bristled at him, even though she could tell that he was teasing her.

He'd better not try coming and living in *her* waters ever again. She'd make sure that Pantani remembered how bad it had been, and so would stop them.

"Good bye," the king said. He paused. He looked as though he wanted to hold out his hand again.

Shawna grit her teeth. She was *not* going to try to curtsey again, damn it! And she didn't care if that was a bad word.

Instead, the king took a bow. He bent almost in half.

Was that a way of showing her respect? She kind of thought it did.

She merely bowed her head in return.

Then the king turned and marched away, the rest of his court following him. The little lights of the Merikin danced beside them, showing him and his people a way out of the water, up back into the light.

Shawna was, but wasn't, sad to see him go. He'd brought many human-like things with him. They'd made her feel more comfortable, before, when she'd been newly dead.

Now, they needed to all be destroyed. So that just the swamp remained.

Shawna slowly swam through the swamp, heading toward the weed forest. She had a favor to ask Pantani, though she wasn't sure the swamp could grant it.

Pantani had magic of a sort, but possibly not like that.

The murky water didn't bother Shawna anymore. She swam easily through it. Though she was no longer swimming like she once did, with a strong breast stroke. She didn't walk, either. She flowed, instead. It was like floating in the water, except she moved herself forward in whatever direction she willed herself to go.

She couldn't believe how dark she'd once thought the swamp was. Now, she saw all the shades of green that made up the weeds growing out of the mud ground. How gracefully the ferns swayed. The rich smell of the water.

Shawna felt *more* of the swamp as well. She realized she was gaining awareness of Pantani's borders. She hadn't met the Russian Olives to the north (not yet!) but she knew where they stood guard. Even if she closed her eyes and spun around, she knew exactly where she floated in terms of the orchard, which direction was North or East.

Pausing, Shawna thought she heard something.

Not part of the swamp song, not the buzzing of the dragonflies or the singing of the blackbirds in their nests above her head.

No, a lighter sound.

Words.

Her name.

Quick as a flash, Shawna turned around and flowed that direction, where the edge of the swamp kissed the orchard.

Toward her sister.

Shawna felt herself growing as she neared the surface. She *had* shrunk—a lot—when she'd gone under the water. She wasn't quite full size when her head crested the surface of the swamp, but she was closer to how big she'd been when she'd died.

She didn't know how many days had passed since she'd first entered the swamp. She didn't need to sleep, and beneath the waters it always seemed to be the same time.

However, between how the air felt, and Rowan's appearance, Shawna would guess that about a month had gone by.

The sun was just going down. Burnt orange and dark purple clouds filled the horizon. Crisp air touched her cheeks, making her shiver. It had to be September, now, no longer August. Autumn was coming, and with it, the coldness of winter. Shawna shivered in the open air, though she only put her head above the water.

Rowan had grown her hair out some. Shawna hoped she'd keep it longer. Her sister looked cuter with longer hair. Though not as long as Shawna's, of course.

Rowan looked tired. Shawna remembered that once, she'd been able to reach her sister, her twin, from deep down under her dreams.

Would she still be able to do that when she became one with the swamp? Would she still want to?

Rowan looked as though she was bathed in the light. Shawna knew her sister wasn't a blonde. She still seemed so much brighter than Shawna.

Maybe it was the swamp mud flowing through Shawna's veins, now, that kept her darker.

Her sister couldn't see her, of course. She'd never been able to see the swamp lights, either.

"Shawna…" Rowan said softly, then stopped.

If Shawna had been alive, she knew she would have felt her heart beating harder.

"I know your body is in the cemetery, with Nana and Gramps," Rowan said. "And Mom goes there to talk with you. Constantly. But Mrs. Thomas—she's the shrink Mom and Dad are sending me to—said I could talk with you anywhere. So I'm coming here."

Yes, yes! Shawna wanted to cry. But she had no words and could only watch in silence.

"I hated you for dying," Rowan said. "For leaving me all alone. For going out and having adventures on your own."

Shawna nodded. If Rowan had died, Shawna would have resented being left behind.

"I thought, for a while, about joining you," Rowan whispered. "Under the waters." She leaned out past the edge of the reeds, looking straight down into the murk.

No! That couldn't just be Rowan, could it? That had to be the king's influence.

How could Shawna keep her sister safe? She rushed forward, coming as close to the border between the swamp and the land as she dared. The edge was like a live wire in the water, making her skin tingle.

"But you'd just yell at me if I did try to join you," Rowan continued, leaning back.

Rowan sighed and wiped away a tear. "So I have to go make my own adventures," she said, nodding. "Though I dream of you, sometimes. And the king's court under the water. The fish people. The mermaids."

Mermaids? There weren't any mermaids in the swamp. Shawna was learning every inch, and there wasn't one of those creatures to be found anywhere.

At least, not now…

"I just…I wanted you to know. That I'm going to stay here. On the land. In the orchard," Rowan said. Her voice still sounded unhappy. She obviously missed Shawna.

Shawna automatically opened her mouth to tell her sister that she missed her as well.

All that came out was a song. A sad song, like what her mom sang sometimes after Gramps, her dad, had died.

But Rowan seemed to hear it anyway. "I know you're there. Watching over the swamp. I'll be here. In the orchard. Among the trees."

Rowan pushed herself up to her knees, then gasped. "Lights! The swamp lights! The lights you always told me about!"

Shawna looked around her. All she saw were the Merikin, slowly approaching the border between the swamp and the orchard.

"Thank you for showing me," Rowan said, tears streaming down her face. "I'll stay on this side of the lights. I promise."

Shawna nodded one last time, watching as her sister left.

It was the best she could hope for. That her sister stayed safe.

Shawna floated on her back on the top of the water, looking up at the stars. She'd seen them wheel around the sky ten thousand times before, back when the waters of the swamp were part of the great inland sea, when the mountains roared, back even when the glaciers came.

She found she could take one, last, deep breath before she sank back down, losing herself and her form as Pantani wrapped itself around her.

And if the swamp had more of an edge, and seemed a little more aware, well, that was just the humans' imagination.

Even if one of them claimed that the swamp always answered her when she spoke.

THE END

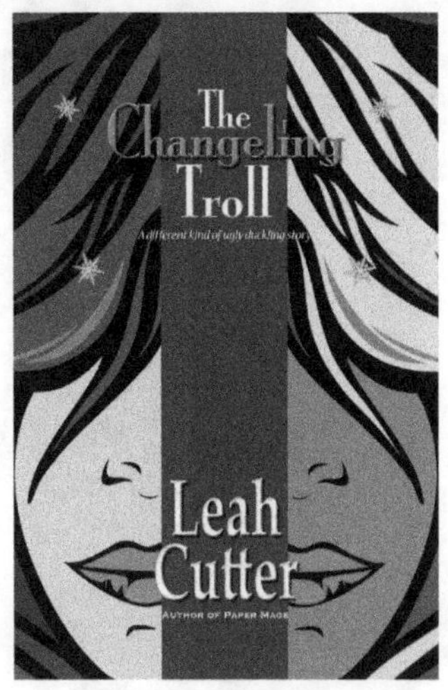

If you enjoyed this story, you'll also enjoy the first two books in the Seattle Trolls trilogy, a new-adult urban fantasy series that turns the ugly duckling myth on its head:

The Changeling Troll
The Princess Troll

About The Author

Leah Cutter writes page-turning fiction in exotic locations, such as a magical New Orleans, the ancient Orient, Hungary, the Oregon coast, rural Kentucky, Seattle, Minneapolis, and many others.

She writes literary, fantasy, mystery, science fiction, and horror fiction. Her short fiction has been published in magazines like Alfred Hitchcock's Mystery Magazine and Talebones, anthologies like Fiction River, and on the web. Her long fiction has been published both by New York publishers as well as small presses.

Read more books by Leah Cutter at www.KnottedRoadPress.com.

Follow her blog at www.LeahCutter.com.

Never miss a release!

If you'd like to be notified of new releases, sign up for my newsletter.

I only send out newsletters once a quarter, will never spam you, or use your email for nefarious purposes. You can also unsubscribe at any time.

http://www.LeahCutter.com/newsletter/

Reviews

It's true. Reviews help me sell more books. If you've enjoyed this story, please consider leaving a review of it on your favorite site.

About Knotted Road Press

Knotted Road Press fiction specializes in dynamic writing set in mysterious, exotic locations.

Knotted Road Press non-fiction publishes autobiographies, business books, cookbooks, and how-to books with unique voices.

Knotted Road Press creates DRM-free ebooks as well as high-quality print books for readers around the world.

With authors in a variety of genres including literary, poetry, mystery, fantasy, and science fiction, Knotted Road Press has something for everyone.

Knotted Road Press
www.KnottedRoadPress.com